S0-AAZ-637

The Bravest of Us All

MARSHA DIANE ARNOLD *pictures by* BRAD SNEED

Dial Books for Young Readers New York

Published by
Dial Books for Young Readers
A division of Penguin Putnam Inc.
345 Hudson Street
New York, New York 10014

Designed by Nancy R. Leo-Kelly
Printed in Hong Kong on acid-free paper
1 3 5 7 9 10 8 6 4 2

Library of Congress Cataloging in Publication Data
Arnold, Marsha Diane.
The bravest of us all/Marsha Diane Arnold;
pictures by Brad Sneed.—1st ed.
p.   cm.
Summary: Ruby Jane thinks that her sister Velma Jean is
the bravest person in her family, but when a tornado comes,
Ruby Jane shows that she is very brave herself.
ISBN 0-8037-2409-8
[1. Courage—Fiction. 2. Sisters—Fiction. 3. Tornadoes—Fiction.
4. Fear—Fiction.] I. Sneed, Brad, ill. II. Title.
PZ7.A7363 Br   2000   [E]—dc21   99-34170   CIP

The full-color artwork was prepared using watercolor
on Soft Press watercolor paper.

When my sister Velma Jean was ten, there was nothin' she was afraid of. Well, almost nothin'. Of us seven brothers and sisters, she was the bravest of us all.

Velma Jean could walk barefoot 'cross the sandbur patch that lay between the house and the barn, just like she was strollin' through a green grass meadow.

The rest of us had to put on shoes or beg Velma Jean to carry us piggy-back if we wanted to see a new litter of kittens in the hayloft.

Velma Jean could swim in the horse tank on the hottest day of summer, even though my older brother, Orville John, swore it was full of biting catfish just waitin' to cut our toes off.

The rest of us had to stand close and wait for Velma Jean's splashes to cool our sweaty faces.

And when dinner was a mite meager, Velma Jean could cross the pasture to the sandhill plum bushes, even when Alfred the Bull was in a fiercesome mood.

The rest of us had to walk up the road and down Mrs. Lecklieder's driveway. By the time we got there, we were starvin' and Velma Jean had already eaten her fill.

When neighbors came to visit, they'd look at Velma Jean
breaking a new colt and say, "Why, Velma Jean, you *are* brave."
And Velma Jean said right back, "I'm the bravest of us all."
Some days I wished I was the bravest of us all, but I was afraid
of most everything.

Every time Old Peddler Jack came to sell his wares, I'd hide
under the bed. Velma Jean walked right over to his buggy and said,
"How-do." I always ended up with dustballs in my hair, while Velma
Jean got a handful of licorice.

Mama said, "Don't worry, Ruby Jane. Velma Jean may be the bravest, but you're the best kitchen helper." Somehow, bein' the best kitchen helper wasn't near as exciting as bein' the bravest. Still, I didn't mind it none helpin' Mama.

Workin' in the kitchen with the smell of risin' bread circling around was a nice way to spend afternoons. And if it got a mite warm, I cooled off in the storm cellar.

Mama called it the root cellar 'cause she used it for storin' root vegetables—jars of beets, potatoes, and carrots. I got to choose the vegetable for supper every night.

Daddy called it the cave because it was cool and quiet down there under the earth. In summer he put boxes of straw on the floor for the hens. I got to collect their eggs every day.

On days when the air was heavy with heat, I'd sit with Old Red and the other hens, soakin' up the coolness of the earth. Sometimes my little sister, Elsie June, would join me. We'd sort through Mama's ol' pickle crock, filled with buttons cut from worn-out clothes. We'd hold the prettiest against our aprons, make-believin' we were fancy ladies.

When Velma Jean walked by, I'd call, "Velma Jean, come get cool."

She'd say, "I got work to do above ground. Besides, I got the horse tank to keep me cool."

So Velma Jean never came into the storm cellar. I always believed it was because she was busy bein' the bravest of us all.

There was no reason for her to go into the storm cellar, anyway. No reason for any of us to, 'cept to collect eggs and choose root vegetables for supper. No storms or tornadoes ever came near our farm. That's because it lay in the bend of Cowskin Creek, and everyone knows tornadoes don't set down in the bend of a creek.

So no one ever knew Velma Jean's secret . . . until the year Cowskin Creek went dry.

The day was hot and sultry. Velma Jean was swimmin' in the horse tank. The rest of us were standin' real close just waitin' for a splash here and there.

"Look at that sky," Henry Joe said. "I've never seen it such a funny green color."

"It's green as the moss in the horse tank," said Elsie June.

"Look at ol' Alfred," said Marvin James. "He and the cows are as noisy as a fox in a henhouse. Stampin' their hooves and mooin' up a storm."

"But everything else is *sooooo* quiet," said Cora Joan.

Suddenly, out of the quiet came a rumble more frightenin' than Preacher Watson's Sunday sermon. Out of the southwest an angry brown cloud pushed down from the light-green sky.

Just then Orville John gathered up Elsie June in his arms. "This storm's not kiddin' and neither am I. See that hawk circlin' in front of the clouds? That means a tornado for sure. Everyone to the storm cellar."

A flash of lightning skedaddled us toward the house. Rain drenched our faces as we headed for the cellar's wooden door. Daddy held it open, countin' us as we stumbled down the steps.

"Six," he said as I ran past him. He should have said seven right after, but he didn't. I thought the wind must have snatched his words away. When I turned around, I knew different. There was no seven. There was no Velma Jean.

"Down the stairs, Ruby Jane," Mama called from below.

I looked back at the horse tank. Velma Jean was huddled beside it. She was the bravest of us all, but she looked small and alone.

Before Daddy could grab me, I pushed my body against the wind and headed back toward the horse tank. When I got there, I reached out my hand to Velma Jean and scrunched down beside her. "Velma Jean," I said, "I know you're brave, but there's a tornado brewin' and it's like to swallow you up."

"If the tornado swallows me, it'll be into the sky," said Velma Jean. "That storm cellar will swallow me into the ground. I'll take my chances with the tornado."

When the wind stopped to catch its breath, I looked into Velma
Jean's face. Tears welled in her eyes when she mentioned that ol'
storm cellar. That's when I knew her secret . . . even the bravest of
us all was scared of somethin'.

"Velma Jean," I said, "you can walk barefoot on sandburs, swim
in the horse tank, and stand up to Alfred. There's no need to be
afraid of an ol' hole in the ground."

"Ruby Jane," she said right back, "when I cross the sandbur patch, I just pretend I'm strollin' through a green grass meadow. And I know there aren't any biting catfish in the horse tank, 'cause Orville John's the biggest kidder this side of Ravanna. And when I cross the meadow with Alfred in a fiercesome mood, well, I can be in just as fiercesome a mood when my mouth is waterin' for those sandhill plums. Besides, I do all those things in the light of day, on top of the earth, where I can see forever."

I peeked around the horse tank and saw a brown funnel cloud stirrin' itself down from the sky.

"You may know about bein' brave, Velma Jean. But I know all about that storm cellar. I promise I won't let it swallow you."

I stood up, held tight to Velma Jean's hand, and looked that tornado in the face. The wind sounded like Old Engine 85 comin' down the railroad tracks. The funnel grew darker and wider, nearly touchin' the ground. It was headin' straight toward us, howlin' like a coyote. I was howlin' too. "I'm not goin' into that cellar without you, Velma Jean."

I never knew if Velma Jean gave in because she was afraid of my bein' blown away or her bein' blown away. Maybe it was some of both.

Down in the storm cellar, Velma Jean sat close beside me, her face as ash green as the sky before the storm. I knew it was more from the closed-in feelin' and the dark corners than the whirlin' tornado above us.

I showed her Mama's pickle crock, filled with buttons. I let her hold one of Old Red's eggs warm against her cheek. It seemed to help a little, but after that day Velma Jean never went into the storm cellar again. 'Course, she never had to, 'cause Cowskin Creek never went dry again, and everyone knows tornadoes don't set down in the bend of a creek.

Velma Jean still walks barefoot over sandburs, swims in the new horse tank, and stands up to Alfred the Bull.

One thing is different, though.

When neighbors come to visit, they look at Velma Jean breaking a new colt and say, "Why, Velma Jean, you *are* brave."

And Velma Jean says right back, "I'm brave. It's true. But let me tell you 'bout the day my little sister Ruby Jane looked a tornado in the face."